This is the story of how a wolf and a sheep fell in love.

It began one night in early spring.

The she-wolf crept like a shadow
down a moonlit hillside.

The lone sheep was unaware, chewing grass
and singing a song. The she-wolf fell in love
with the song first, then the voice,
then the sheep himself.

When she gave him
flowers, he ate them
and then felt sorry.

When he gave her woollen mittens,
she tore them to pieces trying to put them
over her sharp claws.

In time, they got married.

No one came to the wedding,
because neither the flock nor
the pack approved.

But they were happy and they lived together on a grassy hill.

And then, most wonderfully of all...

...they had a son.

He was born with the sharp snout of his mother,
her pointy ears and her long hairy tail... but also
with the soft woolly body of his father.

They called him Woolf.

They were not sure if he
was more lamb or pup.

He chased his tail...

...and hunted the fields
for the sweetest grasses...

...and at night he'd baa at the moon.

He was sheepish after he'd
chewed his mum's slippers...

...and each morning he'd
wolf down the dandelions
his dad prepared for him.

For fun, he often chased his shadow, pouncing on the soft edges of it.

But other times it chased him and he'd have to hide in the shade of the old elm tree to escape its jagged teeth.

Woolf grew up happy, although he was a little lonely.

As he got older, he grazed further and further from his parents – exploring the far sides of distant hills.

It was on one of these wandering days that he met a pack of wolves.

The first thing Woolf noticed was how sleek they all were.
Their dark fur gleamed. Their eyes were fiery orange.

They were magnificent.

"What are you supposed to be?" they asked.

'I'm a... a... wolf," said Woolf.

"But why are you so woolly?"

"I'm in disguise," fibbed Woolf.
"I'm going on a sheep hunt."

The wolves thought Woolf was wonderful.

That night, while his parents were asleep,
Woolf sheared the wool from his body – so that he could
fit in better with the wolves.

The next morning, his parents told him off,
but by then it was too late.

Woolf spent his days with the wolves, pretending to like the things they liked.

It was fantastic, for a while. But soon he got tired of trying to hide the wool that was growing all along his back and on his tummy.

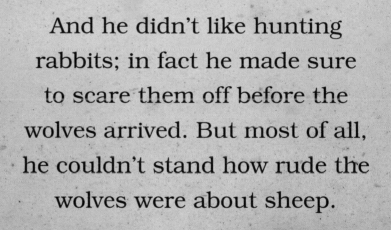

And he didn't like hunting rabbits; in fact he made sure to scare them off before the wolves arrived. But most of all, he couldn't stand how rude the wolves were about sheep.

One morning Woolf decided
not to go back to the wolves.
Instead, he wandered off to
graze in the opposite direction.

Past a stream and
over a hill he met
a flock of sheep.

"What are you supposed to be?" they asked.
The sheep all had such glorious wool, soft as
summer clouds. And they spoke so tenderly.

Woolf thought they were marvellous.

"Oh, I'm a... a... sheep," he replied.

"But why do you have such pointy
ears and such a long bushy tail?"
the sheep asked.

"It's a disguise," lied Woolf,
"so that the wolves won't chase me."

The sheep thought Woolf was wonderful.

That night, while Woolf's parents were out
dancing, he used some of his father's styling
mousse to slick down his wolf ears. He curled his
tail with his mother's curlers and whitened
it with pawfuls of talcum powder.

Woolf knew his parents wouldn't approve of his new look, and so he woke before sunrise, crossed the stream and wandered over the hill to join the flock.

Woolf spent his days with the sheep, pretending to enjoy sheep things. But soon he grew tired of that, too.

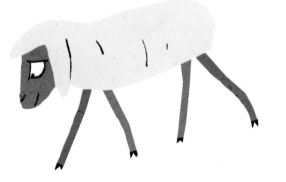

It hurt to have his ears slicked down all day long, and he didn't like the way the sheep just followed each other about aimlessly. Most of all, he couldn't stand how mean the sheep were about wolves.

And so Woolf left the flock.

His mum and dad found him crying
in the shade of the old elm tree.

"What's the matter?" his parents asked.

"I don't belong anywhere – I'm not a wolf
and I'm not a sheep," Woolf sobbed.

"It's true," said his mother,
"you are part wolf and part sheep –
which means you're something new and special."

"If you try to be only a wolf or a sheep," said his dad,
"you'll ignore the other half of who you are, and that
will make you sad."

Today Woolf isn't popular with the
wolves or the sheep. The wolves are
too concerned with wolf things and
the sheep are too concerned
with sheep things.

But Woolf has made new friends.

He is friends
with a horse fly,
and a bullfrog,
and a catfish.

And he is happy.